"A clever retelling of Carroll's classic story with all the imagery of the original." —*The Wishing Shelf*

REVIEW

It is, I think, very important to open the classics to younger children. Although the original texts are, of course, the best, there is still plenty of room for a good retelling, particularly if the story can then be accessed by younger readers.

In this abridgment of Lewis Carroll's popular children's novel, the authors have worked very hard to include many aspects of the original, from the Jabberwocky to Tweedledum and Tweedledee. Also, the imagery of 'chess' is still prominent, as is the 'mirror' theme, i.e. everything seems to be backwards.

I think, all in all, the authors have worked wonders with this retelling. It must be remembered, this is a difficult story in many ways. Carroll, I think, is a rather odd writer who tends not to focus so much on plot, but on setting and character - and, of course, trying to confuse the reader as much as possible. I often wonder if, when he wrote his Alice books, he wasn't enjoying a large number of mind-altering drugs.

But, thankfully, the two authors have persevered. And, by doing so, are offering 7 – 12 year olds a very accessible text. Carroll's word play is still there, as is his logic and, of course, his fantasy. But, with a text of this sort, the young reader now has a chance of understanding it. Well, most of it anyway.

Finally, to the drawings. The illustrator is very talented; VERY talented, helping the reader to picture the characters and to understand Carroll's often surreal settings. Although I enjoyed the story, it was, in fact, the drawings that blew my mind. If I ever write a children's book, I will be turning to Farzana Cooper to illustrate it.

To sum up, this retelling would, I think, would be welcome in any school library. And, if I was trying to help a younger child to access Carroll's work, a book of this nature would be most welcome. Let's face it, it has to be better than the 2016 Johnny Depp film. Now that was terrible!

—A 'Wishing Shelf' Book Review

Through the Looking-Glass

And What Alice Found There

Lewis Carroll

Through the Looking-Glass

And What Alice Found There

Lewis Carroll

Abridged by Fiza Pathan and
Michaelangelo Zane
Illustrated by Farzana Cooper

Fiza Pathan Publishing OPC Private Limited

Mumbai, INDIA

Rare Classics

Imprint. Freedom With Pluralism®
Fiza Pathan Publishing OPC Private Limited
Symbol Apts., Flat No 2, Tertullian Rd, Off Dr. Peter Dias Road, Bandra West, Mumbai 400050, INDIA
Email. fizapathan@fizapathanpublishing.com

Editor. Kimberly Catanzarite.
Illustrator. Farzana Cooper.
Cover art and design: Farzana Cooper and LLPix Photography & Design.

Through the Looking-Glass, And What Alice Found There/ Carroll, Lewis. Abridged by Pathan, Fiza and Zane, Michaelangelo - 1st ed.

ISBN 978-8-1936044-9-6 Hardback
ISBN 978-8-1938201-0-0 Paperback
ISBN 978-8-1938201-1-7 E-book

Through the Looking-Glass, And What Alice Found There

According to Alice, one thing was for certain: The white kitten had nothing to do with the mischief. It was the black kitten's fault entirely.

The white kitten had been having its face washed by Dinah, the old cat, her mother. Being so occupied, it could not have had any hand in the mischief.

It truly had to be the black kitten's fault.

Dinah washed her children's faces in a very interesting way. First, she held the poor thing down by its ears with one paw, and then with the other paw she rubbed its face all over.

Alice sits on the couch with the naughty black kitten on her lap, while Dinah, the mother cat, washes the white kitten's face.

The white kitten who was being cleaned up felt that this was meant for its own good.

The black kitten had been finished with earlier in the afternoon. So, while Alice was sitting curled up in a corner of the great armchair, half talking to herself and half asleep, the black kitten had undone the yarn Alice had been trying to wind up. There it was spread over the hearthrug in all knots and tangles with the kitten running after its own tail in the middle.

"Oh, you wicked little thing," said Alice, grabbing up the kitten and giving it a kiss. "Dinah ought to have taught you better manners."

Alice scrambled back into the armchair, taking the kitten and the yarn with her. She began to wind the ball up again.

She spoke to herself and sometimes to the kitten as she worked.

The next day would be the day of the bonfire, and Alice promised the black kitten they would go to see it.

Alice wound two of three turns of the yarn around the kitten's neck just to see how it would look, but this led to a scramble in which the ball rolled upon the floor, and yards and yards of it unwound once again.

Alice picked up the yarn again, and with the kitten, she settled back in the armchair, murmuring aloud that it was all the kitty's fault. Alice said that the black kitten would be punished immediately, but it so happened that Alice was saving up all its punishments for later.

It was at that very moment Alice wondered whether the adults of the house had also saved up all her punishments. What would they do to her at the end of the year? Prison? Going without dinner for each punishment? Then, when the miserable day came, Alice would have to go without fifty dinners at once.

"Kitty, can you play chess?" asked Alice. "Now, don't smile, my dear, because when we were playing just now you watched just as if you understood it. When I said 'check,' you purred and it was really a very nice check. I might have won if it hadn't been for that nasty knight chess piece."

It was then that Alice declared, "Let's pretend," which was an unusual game that Alice loved to play.

It was her favorite game and her favorite phrase. Once when she said it to her elder sister, "Let's pretend we're kings and queens," her sister, who was always exact, said that there were only two of them. To which Alice replied, "You be one of them, and I shall be all the rest."

And once Alice had really frightened her old nurse by shouting suddenly, "Nurse! Do let's pretend that I'm a hungry hyena and you're a bone!"

Alice giggled. "Let's pretend that you're the Red Queen, kitty!"

Alice wondered about the Looking-Glass House that was reflected in the mirror.

She retrieved the Red Queen chess piece from the chess table and set it up before the kitten as a model for it to imitate. She felt that the procedure, however, was not successful as the kitten wouldn't fold its arms properly. So, to punish the kitten, Alice held it up to the Looking-Glass that it might see how sulky it was. Alice warned the kitten that if it was not good, Alice would pass it through the mirror into the Looking-Glass House.

Alice wondered about the Looking-Glass House that was reflected in the mirror. Would the kitten ever get milk in there? But perhaps Looking-Glass milk was not good to drink.

Alice wondered how would it be to live in a Looking-Glass House.

Suddenly, to Alice, the glass became soft, like gauze, and then turned into a sort of mist.

She immediately climbed up on the mantel and in another moment Alice stepped through the glass.

She jumped lightly down into the Looking-Glass room and looked around.

The room was quite different compared to the one Alice came from on the other side. For instance, the pictures on the wall next to the fire seemed to be alive. The clock on the mantel had the face of a little old man, and he was grinning at Alice.

The glass became soft, like gauze, and Alice immediately climbed up on the mantel and in another moment stepped through the glass.

"They don't keep this room so tidy as the other," said Alice, as she noticed that several of the chess pieces were down in the hearth among the cinders in the grate.

On closer inspection, she realized that the chessmen were alive and walking about in twos. She saw to her amazement the Red King and Red Queen walking together, as well as the White King and White Queen sitting on a shovel near the hearth. Two Castles were also walking arm in arm. However, they seemed not to be able to see Alice. She was invisible where they were concerned.

Suddenly something began squeaking on the chess table behind Alice. One of the White Pawns rolled over and began kicking.

"It is the voice of my child," the White Queen cried out, as she rushed past the King so suddenly that she pushed him in the cinders. The Queen tried in vain to climb up to the crying Pawn.

Alice was very anxious to be of use so she hastily picked up the Queen and set her on the chess table by the side of the noisy little pawn. The Queen gasped and sat down. The rapid journey through the air had given her a fright. For a minute or two she only hugged the baby pawn in silence. As soon as she had recovered her breath, she called out to the White King sitting sulkily among the ashes.

"Mind the volcano!"

On closer inspection, Alice realized that the chessmen were alive and walking about in twos.

"What volcano?" asked the King.

"Blew me up," panted the Queen, who was still a little out of breath. "Mind you come up the regular way and don't get blown up!"

Alice watched the White King as he struggled up from bar to bar. She felt that he would certainly take hours to get up to the table at that rate. So she picked him up very gently, and slower than she had lifted the Queen, so as not to take his breath away. But before she put him on the chess table, she thought she might as well dust him a little as he was covered with ashes.

The poor King was far too astonished to cry out, but his eyes and mouth went on getting larger and larger, and rounder and rounder. Alice almost dropped him to the floor due to her laughing at his reaction to her dusting. After she smoothed his hair and brushed the ashes off him, Alice set him upon the table near the Queen.

But the King lay perfectly flat on his back and didn't move. Alice was alarmed at what she had done and went round the room to see if she could find any water to throw over him. However, other than a bottle of ink, she could find nothing else. She felt that would have to do.

When she returned to the table with the bottle of ink, however, she found that the King had recovered. He and the Queen were talking together in a frightened whisper.

"The horror of that moment," the King said, "I shall never—never forget it!"

"You will, though," the Queen said, "if you don't make a memorandum of it."

Alice then looked on with great interest as the King took an enormous memorandum book out of his pocket and began writing. A sudden thought then struck Alice, and she took hold of the end of the pencil that the King was writing with and began writing for him.

The poor King looked puzzled and unhappy. He struggled with the pencil for some time without saying anything.

"I really must get a thinner pencil," the King said. "I can't manage this one a bit. It writes all manner of things that I don't intend."

The Queen then looked over into the book and saw the line that Alice, the invisible Alice, had written. The sentence was, "The White Knight is sliding down the poker. He balances very badly."

"That's not a memorandum of your feelings," said the Queen.

"But, oh!" thought Alice, jumping up. "If I don't make haste I shall have to go before I've seen what else lies here in this Looking-Glass world."

She then decided to have a look at the garden.

When Alice came out of the house, she felt that she would be able to see the Looking-Glass garden far better if she were to climb up the hill yonder.

So she walked toward the hill, but the path kept on turning at odd angles, and every time Alice tried to make her way up the hill, she landed back at the door of the house.

"How curiously the path twists," she said.

She then took another path wandering up and down and trying turn after turn, but it always led her back to the house no matter what she did.

"Oh, it's too bad," she cried. "I never saw such a house for getting in the way! Never!"

However, there was the hill further away in full sight so there was nothing to be done but to start again. This time, Alice came upon a large flowerbed with a border of daisies and a willow tree growing in the middle.

"Oh, Tiger Lily," said Alice, addressing herself to one that was waving gracefully about in the wind, "I wish you could talk.

"We can talk," said the Tiger Lily, "when there's anybody worth talking to."

Alice was so astonished that she could not speak for a moment. She then very softly and timidly asked, "And can all flowers talk?"

"As well as you can," said the Tiger Lily, "and a great deal louder."

"It isn't good manners for us to speak unless spoken to, you know," said the Rose.

Alice then asked the talking flowers whether they were not frightened, planted out here with no one to care for them as they were.

"There's the tree in the middle. What else is it good for?" the Rose replied.

"But what could it do if any danger came?" asked Alice.

"It could bark," said the Rose.

"It says 'bough-wough,'" cried a Daisy. "That's why its branches are called 'boughs,' didn't you know?"

And here they all began shouting together until the air seemed quite full of shrill little voices.

Alice asked the flowers how they could talk so nicely, to which one of them explained that their flowerbed was hard, whereas in other gardens, on the other side of the Looking-Glass, the beds are made too soft and so the flowers are always asleep.

This sounded like a very good explanation, and Alice was quite pleased to know it. "I never thought of that before!" she said.

"It's my opinion that you never think at all," the Rose said to Alice in a rather severe tone.

It was then that Alice asked, "Are there any other people in the garden besides me?"

"There's one other flower in the garden that can move about like you," said the Rose.

Alice curtsied before the Red Queen.

"Is she like me?" Alice asked excitedly, for the thought crossed her mind that there could have been another little girl in the garden somewhere.

The Rose continued, "Well, she has the same awkward shape as you, but she's redder and her petals are shorter and she wears her nine pins all around her head.

Alice looked around eagerly and found that it was the Red Queen that the Rose spoke of. Alice realized that the Red Queen had grown a good deal, for when Alice first saw her on the hearth, she had been only three inches high. Now the Red Queen was half a head taller than Alice herself.

"I think I'll go and meet her," said Alice, for although the flowers were interesting enough, she felt that it would be far grander to have a talk with a real queen.

So, Alice set off from the flowerbed to meet the Red Queen, and she had not been walking a minute before she found herself face-to-face with the Queen and in full sight of the aforementioned hill she had been aiming at for so long.

"Where do you come from?" asked the Red Queen. "And where are you going? Look up, speak nicely and don't twiddle your fingers all the time.

Alice obeyed the Queen and began to explain that she had lost her way to which the Red Queen declared, "I don't know what you mean by your way, as all ways about here belong to me." Then in a kinder tone she asked Alice to curtsey.

Alice wondered a little about this, but she was too much in awe of the Queen to do anything else.

"It's time for you to answer now—open your mouth a little wider when you speak and always say, 'Your Majesty,'" the Queen ordered as she looked at her time-piece.

"I only wanted to see what the garden was like, Your Majesty," said Alice.

Then the Red Queen patted her on the head, which Alice did not like at all, and they walked on in silence until they reached the top of the hill. Alice looked in all directions over the country, which had a number of tiny brooks running straight across it from side to side. The ground between was divided up in squares by a number of little green hedges that reached from brook to brook.

"I declare, it's marked out just like a large chess-board," exclaimed Alice. Then she noticed that just like a chessboard there were men moving about in each square.

Alice's heart began to beat quick with excitement as she said, "It's a great huge game of chess that's being played. How I wish I was one of them! I wouldn't mind being a pawn, though of course I should like to be a queen best."

"I declare, it's marked out just like a large chessboard," exclaimed Alice.

Alice glanced rather shyly at the Red Queen as she said this, but her companion only smiled pleasantly.

"That's easily managed," the Queen said, "when you get to the eighth square, you'll be a queen."

Suddenly they began to run. Alice could not quite make out how it was that they began. All she remembered was they were running hand in hand and the Red Queen went so fast that it was all she could do to keep up with her.

The Red Queen kept crying, "Faster! Faster!"

The most curious part of the whole thing was that the trees and the other things round them never changed their places at all, however fast they went.

This puzzled Alice quite a bit, but the Red Queen kept on saying, "Faster! Don't try to talk."

They went so fast that they seemed to skim through the air, hardly touching the ground with their feet, until all at once they stopped and Alice found herself sitting on the ground, breathless and giddy.

The Red Queen propped Alice against a tree and said kindly, "You may rest a little now."

Alice looked around and realized that despite all of the running, they had been in the same place the whole time.

The Red Queen removed a little box out of her pocket and took out a biscuit. "Here, have a biscuit," she said in a good-natured manner.

The Red Queen then said that she would give Alice the directions the rest of the way to the eighth square.

Alice thought it would not be civil to say no, though a biscuit certainly couldn't quench her thirst, but she still took it and ate it as well as she could. The biscuit, however, was very dry, and Alice felt choked as she tried to eat it.

The Red Queen then said that she would give Alice the directions the rest of the way to the eighth square. She offered Alice another biscuit to refresh herself, but Alice refused this time.

"Thirst quenched, I hope?" asked the Red Queen. Alice didn't know at all what to say, but luckily the Queen did not wait for an answer.

"So, you'll go very quickly through the Third Square by railway, and you'll find yourself in the Fourth Square in no time, which belongs to Tweedledum and Tweedledee. The Fifth Square is mostly water; the Sixth belongs to Humpty Dumpty; the Seventh Square is all forest, but one of the Knights will show you the way; and in the Eighth Square we shall be queens together!"

Alice, at the end of the long dialogue, curtseyed and then the Red Queen was gone as quickly as she had come. Whether she vanished into the air or ran quickly into the wood, there was no way of guessing, but the bottom line was that the Red Queen had gone, and Alice knew that she was a Pawn in the chess game and that sooner or later she would have to make her first move.

Of course, Alice thought that the first thing to do was to make a grand survey of the country that she was going to travel through. She felt it was very much like learning geography. She thought of this as she stood on tiptoe in the hope of being able to see a little further.

She ran down the hill and jumped over the first of the six little brooks when she realized she was now in a railway carriage.

"Tickets please!" said the Guard, putting his head in at the window.

All kinds of people and creatures occupied the railway carriage, and they presented their respective tickets.

The Guard then turned to Alice. "Now then! Show your ticket, child!" he said impatiently.

"I'm afraid I haven't got one," Alice said in a frightened tone. "There wasn't a ticket office where I got on."

"Don't make excuses," said the Guard. "You should have bought one from the Engine Driver."

Alice found all of this quite silly and so she thought to herself, "Then there's no use of talking."

"Tickets please!" said the Guard, putting his head in at the window.

And all this time, the Guard was looking at her, first through a telescope, then through a microscope and then through an opera glass. At last he declared, "You're traveling the wrong way." He then shut the window and went away.

"A child ought to know which way she's going even if she doesn't know her name," said the gentleman sitting opposite Alice. He was dressed in white paper.

A Goat that was sitting next to the gentleman in white said in a loud voice, "She ought to know her way to the ticket office even if she doesn't know her alphabet."

And after that, other voices joined in. Alice thought to herself, "What a number of people there are in the railway carriage!"

Then the gentleman in white paper leaned forward and whispered in Alice's ear, "Don't mind what everyone is saying, but if you buy a ticket, be sure to purchase a return ticket every time the train stops."

Alice was quite irritated upon hearing this nonsense. "Indeed, I shan't," Alice said rather impatiently, "I don't belong to this railway journey at all. In fact, I was in the wood and I wish I could get back there."

A shrill scream from the engine drowned everyone's words, and all the passengers, including Alice, jumped in alarm.

A Horse who had put his head out of the window quickly said, "It's only a brook that the train has to jump over."

In another moment, Alice felt the carriage rise straight up into the air.

A Horse who had put his head out of the window quickly said, “It’s only a brook that the train has to jump over.”

Everyone in the carriage seemed satisfied with this, though Alice felt a little nervous at the idea of trains actually jumping, over a brook.

“However, it’ll take us to the Fourth Square and that’s some comfort,” she said to herself.

In another moment, she felt the carriage rise straight up into the air and in her fright, she caught at the thing nearest to her hand which happened to be the Goat’s beard. But the beard seemed to melt away as she touched it. Alice found herself sitting quietly under a tree while the Gnat, who was one of the creatures conversing with her on the railway carriage, balanced itself on a twig just over her head while fanning her with its wings.

Alice was surprised to see that the Gnat was the size of a chicken. Suddenly, the Gnat began to talk about the different insects found in the Looking-Glass world.

The Gnat informed Alice that halfway up a bush she would be able to see a Rocking-horse-fly. If she looked carefully, she would realize that it was made entirely of wood.

“What does it live on?” asked Alice with great curiosity.

“Sap and sawdust,” replied the Gnat.

Alice saw a Rocking-horse-fly, a dragonfly, a Gnat, and a butterfly.

Alice looked at the Rocking-horse-fly with great interest and realized that it must have just been repainted as it looked so bright and sticky.

The Gnat then told her to look at another branch above her head and there she would behold a Snap-dragon-fly with its body made up of plum pudding, its wings of holly leaves, and its head a raisin brimming in brandy.

"And what does it live on?" Alice asked as before.

"Frumenty and mince pie," the Gnat replied. "And it makes its nest in a Christmas box."

Then the Gnat informed Alice that crawling at her feet was a Bread-and-Butter-fly, whose wings were thin slices of bread and butter, its body a crust and its head a lump of sugar.

"And what does it live on?" asked Alice, yet again.

"Weak tea with cream in it," said the Gnat.

On hearing this, a new difficulty came into Alice's head. "Supposing it couldn't find any?"

"Then it would die of course," declared the Gnat.

"But that must happen very often," Alice remarked.

"It always happens," said the Gnat.

After this Alice sat there silent for a minute or two pondering. In another moment her companion, the Gnat, sighed itself away. When Alice looked up, there was nothing whatever to be seen on the twig. She was getting quite chilly with sitting still so long that she got up and walked on.

Alice very soon came to an open field with a wood on the far side of it. It looked much darker than the last wood she'd entered. She felt a little timid about going into it. However, she made up her mind to go on. She definitely couldn't turn back now and she so wanted to get to the Eighth Square and become a queen.

Unfortunately, the moment Alice entered the wood she started to forget the names of things. She forgot what a "tree" was called. She forgot what "forgetting" was called, and shocking of all, she even forgot her own name, though she thought maybe her name began with the alphabet *L*, which was quite funny because it was wrong. Indeed, Alice had entered the wood "where things have no names."

As Alice was trying to remember her own name, a Fawn came wandering by. It looked at Alice with its large gentle eyes, but it didn't seem at all frightened.

"Here then! Here then!" Alice said, as she held out her hand and tried to stroke it.

"What do you call yourself?" the Fawn asked at last and it truly had a soft, sweet voice.

Alice thought, but simply couldn't remember her name. Then a thought struck her and she in turn asked the Fawn, "Please, would you tell me what you call yourself? I think that might help a little."

Alice holds the fawn lovingly in her arms in the 'wood of forgetfulness'.

The Fawn replied, it did not know, but if Alice came along with it further on, it would remember. So they walked on together through the wood, Alice with her arms lovingly holding the Fawn until they came out into another open field. Here the Fawn bounded suddenly forward shaking itself free from Alice's arms.

"I'm a Fawn!" it cried out in a voice of delight. "And dear me! You're a human child!" A sudden look of alarm came into its beautiful brown eyes, and it darted away at full speed.

Alice was vexed at having lost her dear little fellow traveler so suddenly.

"However," she said, "I know my name now and that's some comfort. Alice—Alice—I mustn't forget it again."

Alice was hoping that she would get to the Eighth Square before it got dark, when in the middle of the next wood, she came upon two fat little men.

The two men were standing under a tree each with an arm round the other's neck. On one's collar was printed the word *Dum* and the other *Dee*, and that was how Alice knew that they were Tweedledum and Tweedledee. They stood so still that she quite forgot they were alive, when Tweedledum suddenly said, "If you think we are made of wax, then you can stare at us and pay for the staring."

"Or," continued Tweedledee, "if you think we are alive, you ought to speak to us."

"I'm sure, I'm very sorry," said Alice. "Can you please tell me which is the best way out of the wood as it's getting so dark."

But the fat little men only laughed at each other and grinned. Alice felt that they looked completely like schoolboys. The men then held out both their hands for Alice to shake. She did not wish to upset either of them so she put out both her right and left hand, and shook their hands together at the same time.

Suddenly they all, hand in hand, started dancing round in a ring, and music started to play. Alice felt that the sudden music came from the tree.

They danced for a while, singing, "Here we go round the mulberry bush," when Tweedledee and Tweedledum, being fat, stopped as they were soon out of breath. Then they let go of Alice's hands and stood looking at her for a minute. There was a rather awkward pause as Alice didn't know how to begin a conversation with people she had just been dancing with.

Tweedledee asked Alice, "You like poetry?"

"Yes," said Alice hesitantly. "Pretty well—some poetry."

Tweedledee and Tweedledum.

It was then that Tweedledee and Tweedledum used verse to tell Alice the story of "The Walrus and the Carpenter." Apparently, once when both the sun and the moon were shining in the sky, two friends, one of whom was a well-dressed Walrus and the other a Carpenter, were walking down the beach complaining to themselves most tearfully about such a quantity of sand. There was so much sand present on the beach, they debated whether seven maids, with seven mops, sweeping the sand for half a year, would be able to get the seashore clear of sand. On their walk, the Walrus and the Carpenter came across some Oysters whom the conniving Walrus subtly tempted to come for a walk with the two of them. With fine, but completely nonsense words, the Walrus tempted the young, naïve oysters to leave their Oyster bed. They went along with them only to be eaten by the Walrus and the Carpenter in the end.

"I like the Walrus best," said Alice, at the end of the recitation. "Because he felt a little sorry for the poor Oysters."

"He ate more than the Carpenter though," said Tweedledee.

"That was mean!" Alice said indignantly. "Then I liked the Carpenter best."

"But he ate as many as he could get," said Tweedledum.

This was a puzzler for Alice, and she ended the topic by deciding that both the Walrus and the Carpenter were very unpleasant creatures. Alice's thoughts were interrupted immediately by a sound like the puffing of a large steam engine.

"It's only the Red King snoring," said Tweedledee, when they saw that the sound alarmed Alice.

The brothers each took one of Alice's hands and led her up to where the King was sleeping.

When they reached the place where he was sleeping, Tweedledum said, "Isn't he a lovely sight?"

Alice couldn't say honestly that he was, as he wore a tall red nightcap with a tassel, and he was lying crumpled up into a sort of untidy heap, snoring very loudly.

Alice was very anxious to get out of the wood as she saw that the wood was getting darker and darker. Alice asked the brothers, Tweedledee and Tweedledum, whether they thought it could rain. Tweedledum immediately spread a large umbrella over himself and his brother.

However, when Tweedledum saw a broken toy rattle under a tree, he began to stamp about wildly and tear his hair.

"It's only a rattle, not a rattlesnake," Alice said, after careful examination of the thing, "and it's old and quite broken too."

But however much Alice tried to calm Tweedledum, he remained in a great fury as the rattle was his and was also newly bought.

"It's new I tell you," yelled Tweedledum. "My nice NEW RATTLE!"

During all this, Tweedledee was trying his best to fold up the umbrella with himself in it, until only his head popped out through the closed umbrella, making him seem more like a fish than a human to Alice.

The brothers started getting ready to fight a battle over the topic of the broken rattle. Alice was put in charge of getting them suited for the battle. The poor girl had to dress, tape, and pin various things, like bolsters, blankets, hearth rugs, tablecloths, dish covers, and coal saddles to make up a suit of armor of the most ridiculous kind for each of the brothers. Alice felt that she had never seen such a fuss made about such an insignificant thing in her life.

After they both were fully dressed, Tweedledum said that he had a headache and Tweedledee said that he had a toothache, and so they decided to fight from half past four till six o'clock with Alice watching them, and then they would go for dinner.

"And all this about a rattle!" Alice exclaimed exasperatedly.

At this point, a sort of black object in the sky which seemed like a large crow, started flapping its wings toward them. The two brothers took to their heels and were out of sight in a minute, while Alice remained in the middle of the gusty breeze, where she saw a shawl being blown toward her.

Alice caught the shawl and looked about for the owner, and in another moment the White Queen came running wildly through the wood with both arms stretched out wide as if she were flying. Alice stopped her and gave back her shawl.

"I'm very glad I happened to catch it," Alice said, as she helped the White Queen to put it on again. "Dear me, what a bad state your hair is in!"

"The brush has got entangled in it," the Queen said with a sigh. "And I lost the comb yesterday."

Alice carefully released the brush and did her best to get the Queen's hair in order.

"Come, you look rather better now!" Alice said, after pinning the White Queen's hair. "But really you should have a lady's maid."

"I'm sure I'll take you with pleasure!" the White Queen said. "Two pence a week and jam every other day."

Alice laughed at this and told the Queen she didn't care for jam.

The Queen proceeded to stick a large piece of plaster on her finger and bound the plaster round with a bit of ribbon. A few moments later she began screaming loudly, "My finger's bleeding! Oh! Oh! Oh! Oh!"

"Have you pricked your finger?" Alice asked anxiously.

The Queen replied, "I haven't pricked it yet, but I soon shall. Oh! Oh! Oh!"

"When do you expect to do it?" Alice asked, feeling very much inclined to laugh. But in a moment's time as the White Queen was screaming, the brooch pinned to her shawl flew open and the Queen clutched at it wildly.

"Take care, or you'll hurt yourself," cried Alice, but it was too late. The pin slipped and the Queen pricked her finger, and only then did she stop screaming. According to Alice, all of this was very, very peculiar.

"How old are you?" asked the White Queen.

"I'm seven and a half exactly," replied Alice.

"I'm just one hundred and one, five months, and a day old," declared the Queen.

"I can't believe that!" said Alice.

"Can't you?" the Queen said in a pitying tone of voice.

Alice laughed, "There's no use trying as one can't believe impossible things."

"I feel you haven't had much practice," said the White Queen. She then said that when she was Alice's age, she practiced believing in impossible things for half an hour a day.

Alice crossed a little brook after the Queen. She then looked at the Queen, who she thought seemed to have wrapped herself up in some wool. Alice rubbed her eyes and realized she was no longer with the White Queen, but in a very dark little shop and—was it really a sheep that was sitting on the other side of the counter?

Indeed, leaning with her elbows on the counter was a very old Sheep sitting in an armchair, knitting, and every now and then stopping to take a look at Alice through a great pair of spectacles.

"What is it that you want to buy?" asked the Sheep.

"May I look around first?" asked Alice gently.

"You may look in front of you and on both sides of you if you like," said the Sheep. "But you can't look all round you unless you've got eyes at the back of your head."

The shop seemed to be full of all manner of things. The oddest thing was that the Sheep was knitting with fourteen pairs of needles.

Alice couldn't help but look at the Sheep in astonishment. "She gets more and more like a porcupine every minute," she thought to herself.

"Can you row?" asked the Sheep, handing a pair of knitting needles to Alice.

"What is it that you want to buy?" asked the Sheep.

Suddenly the knitting needles in Alice's hands turned into oars, and Alice found that she and the Sheep were in a little boat, gliding along between banks, so there was nothing else to do but row. However, as Alice continued to row she realized that there was something very peculiar about the water. Every now and then the oars would get stuck in it and they hardly came out again.

A little later, Alice got excited. "Oh look," she exclaimed, "There are some scented rushes and they are such beauties. If you don't mind, can you stop the boat for a minute so that I can pick some?"

"How can I stop it?" said the Sheep. "If you stop rowing, the boat will stop by itself."

Soon the boat drifted downstream and glided among the waving rushes. Alice rolled up her sleeves and her little arms were plunged in elbow deep to get hold of the rushes. She forgot entirely about the Sheep knitting in the boat.

No sooner had Alice collected some wonderfully scented rushes than her booty started to melt away and the blade of one of the oars got stuck in the water and didn't come out again.

"Oh – Oh – Oh!" came a cry from poor Alice, as she was swept straight off her seat and fell right down among the heap of rushes. But she wasn't a bit hurt. She got right up and found this very astonishing.

The Sheep again called out, "Plenty of choices, only make up your mind. Now what do you want to buy?"

Before Alice knew it, they were back in the dark old shop again with the Sheep knitting behind the counter.

"What do you want to buy?" repeated the Sheep once again.

"I should like to buy an egg please," Alice announced timidly. "How much?"

"Five pence farthing for one and two pence for two," the Sheep replied.

Alice found it rather silly that one egg should cost more money than two eggs, but she decided to buy one egg only. "They mightn't be at all nice, you know," she thought to herself.

The Sheep took the money, went to the other end of the shop, and set the egg upright on a shelf. And the egg started to grow larger.

The egg continued to grow larger and larger, and more and more human like.

Alice crossed over another brook as she backed up and stared quite astonished at the egg. It began to develop eyes and a nose and mouth—and then she realized that the egg was Humpty Dumpty himself!

Humpty Dumpty was sitting with his legs crossed on top of a high wall.

Humpty Dumpty was sitting with his legs crossed on top of a high wall. The wall was so narrow that Alice wondered how Humpty Dumpty kept his balance. At first, he didn't take the least notice of her, so she thought he might be a stuffed figure.

"And how exactly like an egg he is!" she said aloud.

"It's very provoking," Humpty Dumpty said quite angrily, "to be called an egg!"

"I said you only looked like an egg, Sir," Alice gently explained. "And some eggs are very pretty you know," she added, hoping to turn her remark into a sort of compliment.

Then Humpty Dumpty asked Alice what her name was. When he heard her say her name was Alice, he got even more angry.

"It's a stupid name as it is. By the way," Humpty Dumpty said. "What does it mean?"

When Alice didn't give an answer, Humpty Dumpty explained that all names must mean something, just like his meant the shape he was. "And a good handsome shape it is too," said Humpty Dumpty with a short laugh. "With a name like yours, you might be any shape!"

"Don't you think you'd be safer down on the ground?" Alice went on in her good-natured way, as she was really getting worried that he might fall at any time. "That wall is so narrow!'

"I don't think so," Humpty Dumpty declared defiantly. "And even if I did fall—I mean," he hesitated, "if I did happen to fall, the King told me—"

"That he would send all his horses and all his men," Alice interrupted rather unwisely, for hearing that, Humpty Dumpty decided that Alice must be some sort of a spy. To that Alice stated that the nursery rhyme was written in a book.

Although Humpty Dumpty wasn't pleased about that either, he offered to shake hands with Alice as he grinned from ear to ear and leaned forward. Alice watched him very worriedly as she shook his hand.

"Yes," explained Humpty Dumpty, "the King has promised that if I were to fall he would send all his horses and all his men to my rescue."

To change the topic, Alice said, "What a beautiful belt you've got on! Or is it a cravat? No it's a belt," she corrected herself. "No it's a cravat."

As she realized what a mistake she had made, Humpty Dumpty went into a great rage and in the end declared that it was a shame a seven-year-old girl like her did not know the difference between a cravat and a belt. He then stated that what he was wearing was a cravat. "It's a cravat that has been gifted to me by the White King and Queen," said Humpty Dumpty proudly. "They gave it to me as an 'unbirthday' present."

"What's an 'unbirthday' present?" asked Alice curiously.

Humpty Dumpty made Alice remove her memorandum book and do a subtraction sum.

$$365 - 1 = 364$$

He said that a person had only one birthday in a year and the remaining 364 days were "unbirthday" days. "And that's how people have unbirthdays as well."

Once Alice was through with the subtraction sum, Humpty Dumpty took the book from her and looked at it carefully.

"You are holding the book upside down," Alice said gently.

"To be sure, I was indeed," said Humpty Dumpty, as Alice turned it around for him. He then mentioned that he had wondered why the sum was looking so queer. Humpty Dumpty declared that the sum done was quite correct and in that way a person on this side of the Looking-Glass could get many presents on 364 "unbirthday" days.

"I had some poetry read out to me," said Alice. "It was 'The Walrus and the Carpenter' narrated by Tweedledee and Tweedledum."

"As regards poetry," said Humpty Dumpty stretching out one of his great hands, "I can repeat a poem to you as well."

Poor Alice didn't want to listen to more poetry, but since he was going to all the trouble to amuse her, she decided that she might as well sit down and listen to him.

Humpty Dumpty began to narrate some lines of poetry, and Alice kept interrupting him with phrases like, "Thank you very much," and "I will write the poem if I can remember it. It is very long."

Humpty Dumpty thus became irritated and warned her not to go on making such remarks. He however, continued his poem, which was quite an unusual one about fishes and kettles and shouting in a messenger's ear, when suddenly and abruptly, Humpty Dumpty ended the poem midway.

"Is that all?" Alice timidly asked.

"That's all," said Humpty Dumpty gruffly. "Now, goodbye."

For Alice, this was quite sudden, but she got the hint she had to be going. She shook hands one last time with Humpty Dumpty, saying a goodbye to him. Alice waited a minute to see if he would speak again, but he didn't, so she quietly continued away, turning her back to him. Soon, however, she heard a loud crash that shook the forest from end to end.

In a moment soldiers came running through the wood in such crowds that they seemed to fill the whole forest. Alice was quite sure that in all her life she had never seen soldiers so uncertain on their feet. They were all tripping, and whenever one went down, several more fell over him so that the ground was covered with heaps of men.

Then came the horses, but they too were stumbling, and whenever the horse stumbled, the rider fell off instantly.

It was at this time that Alice found the White King seated on the ground, busily writing in his memorandum book.

"How many of my soldiers did you see?" the King asked Alice.

"Several thousand I think," she answered quite amazed.

"Four thousand two hundred and seven—that is the exact number," said the King, referring to his memorandum book. Alice then looked ahead and to her astonishment she could see someone coming up the road. The White King declared it was one of his messengers named Haigha, and he pronounced it so as to rhyme with *mayor*. Alice found Haigha a very queer messenger. First of all, he was not running toward them but moving very slowly. Secondly, as he came toward them, he kept on skipping up and down and wriggling like an eel, and his hands were spread out like fans on either side.

The White King told Alice that he had another messenger named Halta. He said he needed two messengers, one to come and one to go.

"I don't understand," said Alice quite confused. "Why one to come and one to go?"

But by this time the messenger reached them, and he was quite out of breath. The King introduced him to Alice and then asked the messenger for a ham sandwich. The messenger, to Alice's great amusement, opened a bag that hung round his neck and handed a sandwich to the King, who devoured it greedily.

"Another sandwich!" said the King.

"There's nothing but hay left now," the messenger said peeking into the bag.

"Hay then," said the King, and he started to eat the hay, which revived him quite a bit.

The whole scene amused Alice very much.

"They're at it again," said the messenger Haigha, screaming into the White King's ears.

"Who are at it again?" asked Alice.

"Why the Lion and the Unicorn, of course!" said the King. "They are fighting for the crown, and the joke of the matter is that it is my crown that they are fighting for all the while."

The three of them hurried off to see the fight.

"Does the one who wins get the crown?" Alice asked as she ran alongside of them, but the White King did not give her a sensible answer.

They came in sight of a great crowd in the middle of which the Lion and the Unicorn were fighting. They were in such a cloud of dust that at first Alice could not make out which was which, but she soon managed to distinguish the Unicorn by his horn.

They placed themselves next to where Halta, the second messenger was standing and watching the fight, with a cup of tea in one hand and a piece of bread and butter in the other.

"He's just been released from prison, and he hadn't finished his tea when he was sent in," Haigha whispered to Alice.

Turning to Halta he shouted, "Speak, can't you?"

But Halta only munched away and drank some more tea.

"Speak, Halta," ordered the White King, "and tell us how the Lion and the Unicorn are getting on with the fight."

Halta made a great effort to speak and also swallowed a large piece of bread and butter. He said, "They're getting on very well. Each of them has been down about ninety-seven times."

There was a pause in the fight, and the Lion and the Unicorn sat down panting while the King called out for a ten-minute break and refreshments. Haigha and Halta set to work at once, carrying round trays of white and brown bread. Alice took a piece to taste, but it was very dry.

"I don't think they'll fight anymore today," said the King, and so he ordered Halta to go and order the drums to begin.

Alice spotted the White Queen running across the country. The White King declared that maybe the White Queen was running away from an enemy who was after her.

"But aren't you going to help her?" Alice asked, very much surprised at his taking things so quietly.

"No use, no use," said the King. "She runs so fearfully quick, but I'll write about it in my memorandum book." At that, the King took out his memorandum book and began to write in it. "Do you spell *creature* with a double *e*," he asked Alice while he wrote.

At this moment, the Unicorn came toward them and his eye happened to fall upon Alice. He stared at her with an expression of deep disgust. "What is this?" he asked at last, pointing at Alice.

"This is a child!" Haigha replied eagerly, coming in front of Alice to introduce her.

The Unicorn declared, "I always thought they were fabulous monsters." The Unicorn looked dreamily at Alice and ordered her to talk. At that, Alice could not help but smile as she began, "Do you know, I always thought Unicorns were fabulous monsters too! I never saw one alive before."

"Well now that we've seen each other," the Unicorn declared, "if you believe in me, I'll believe in you. Is that a bargain?"

"Yes!" replied Alice joyfully.

"Come, fetch out the plum cake, old man," said the Unicorn to the White King. The King beckoned to Haigha to open his bag, and Haigha took a large cake out of it and gave it to Alice to hold while he got out a dish and carving knife.

How they all came out of that small bag, Alice couldn't guess. "It is just like a magic trick," she thought to herself.

The Lion had joined them while this was going on. He looked very sleepy, and his eyes were half shut. "What's this?" he said when he saw Alice.

"You'll never guess. I couldn't myself!" replied the Unicorn.

The Lion looked at Alice wearily, yawning at every word. "Are you an animal, vegetable, or mineral?"

The White King sat between the Unicorn and the Lion. He was very uncomfortable, but there was no other place for him.

The Lion and the Unicorn both eyed the King's crown slyly, and because of that the poor King was frightened and trembling terribly.

"I should win easily," said the Lion, looking at the crown.

"I'm not so sure of that," said the Unicorn.

The Lion began to grumble, as Alice was having an awful time cutting up the cake.

Indeed, she had seated herself on the bank of a little brook with the great dish on her knees and was sawing away diligently with the knife. She was getting quite upset. No matter how much she tried to cut the pieces, they would always join again.

"You don't know how to manage Looking-Glass cakes," the Unicorn remarked. "You must hand it round first and cut it afterward."

To Alice, this sounded like nonsense, but she very obediently got up and carried the dish round and the cake divided itself into three pieces as she did so.

The Unicorn complained that Alice had given a bigger slice to the Lion, but the Lion backed her up by saying that Alice hadn't kept any cake for herself.

It was then that the drums began, and Alice had to put her hands over her ears to shut out the dreadful uproar.

After a while, the noise gradually died down, until at last there were dead silence. Alice lifted her head with some alarm. She thought that maybe she had only dreamed about the Lion and the Unicorn. But then she saw the empty dish of plum cake still lying at her feet, and she reasoned that it was not a dream after all.

At that moment, a loud shouting interrupted her thoughts. A Knight dressed in crimson red armor came galloping down upon her with a great club in his hand.

"You're my prisoner!" the Knight cried, as he tumbled off his horse.

Then suddenly another Knight dressed in White came toward them, tumbling off his horse just as the Red Knight had done

"She's my prisoner, you know!" the Red Knight said.

"Yes, but then I came and rescued her!" the White Knight declared.

"Well, we must fight for her then," said the Red Knight. He and the other Knight took up their helmets, which hung from their saddles and were the shape of a horse's head, and put them on.

They then began their battle by banging away at each other with such fury that Alice hid behind a tree, clear of their blows. Alice noticed that when one of the Knights knocked the other off, he would also tumble off himself, and moreover both Knights mostly fell on their heads.

The short skirmish ended with both of them falling off their horses and landing side by side on the ground. When they got up again, they shook hands and the Red Knight mounted his horse and galloped off.

"It was a glorious victory, wasn't it?" said the White Knight, as he again sat panting upon his horse.

"I don't know," Alice said doubtfully. "I don't want to be anybody's prisoner. I want to be a Queen."

"So you will when you cross the next brook," said the White Knight. "I'll see you safe to the end of the wood and then I must go back, you know, as that will be the end of my move."

The White Knight, with Alice's help, took off his helmet and began to move away. Alice thought she had never seen such a strange-looking soldier in all her life. He was scruffy and kept on tumbling off his horse all the time as they moved along to their destination. The Knight also had certain queer things attached to his saddle, like a beehive, a mousetrap, and carrots. There were anklets around the feet of the White Knight's horse. When Alice asked the White Knight what they were for, he said they were there to guard against the bites of sharks. Alice thought all this to be very peculiar.

"What's that dish for back there?" asked the White Knight, pointing to the empty dish.

"It was meant for plum cake," answered Alice.

The White Knight said, "Help me to get it into this bag of mine. We'd better take the dish with us, in case we find any plum cake."

This took a long time to manage, for although Alice held the bag open very carefully, the Knight was so very awkward in putting in the dish, that the first two or three times he tried, he himself fell into the bag instead.

"It's rather a tight fit, you see," he said, as they got it in at last and once again continued their journey. Through most of the way, the White Knight kept falling off his horse, and Alice had to help him back up each time.

"I'm afraid you've not had much practice in riding," Alice ventured to say, as the Knight scrambled back into the saddle, holding on to Alice's hair with one hand, to save himself from falling over on the other side.

The Knight looked very surprised. "What makes you say that?" he asked.

"Because people don't fall off their horses quite so often when they've had practice," declared Alice.

"I've had plenty of practice," the Knight said very gravely. "Plenty of practice!"

They went on a little way in silence after this, the Knight with his eyes shut muttering to himself and Alice watching anxiously for the next tumble.

"The great art of riding," the Knight suddenly began in a loud voice, "is to keep your balance properly, like this."

He let go of the bridle and stretched out both his arms to show Alice what he meant. This time he fell flat on his back right under the horse's feet.

"Plenty of practice!" he went on repeating all the time that Alice was getting him on his feet again. "Plenty of practice!"

"It is too ridiculous," cried Alice, losing all her patience. "You ought to have a wooden horse on wheels, as that is all you are fit for."

Then the White Knight asked Alice foolishly whether the wooden horse went on more smoothly than a regular horse, to which Alice couldn't help but laugh aloud.

The Knight informed Alice that he was a great inventor of ideas and things. "When I fell just now," he said, "I invented a way of getting over a gate. Would you like to hear it?"

"Very much indeed," Alice said politely.

He went on to describe a most tedious and ridiculous way of getting over a gate, by using one's head first to balance on the gate post and then the legs.

"Don't you think it would be rather hard," asked Alice, quite unsure of herself and the method of getting over the gate.

"I haven't tried it yet," he said gravely, "but yes, I guess it would be a little hard."

He raised his hands in some excitement as he said this and instantly rolled out of the saddle and fell headlong into a deep ditch.

Alice ran to the side of the ditch to look for him. She was startled by the fall, and this time she was afraid he might really be hurt. However, though she could see nothing but the soles of his feet, she was relieved to hear that he was talking on in his usual tone.

"How can you go on talking so quietly, head downward?" Alice asked the Knight, as she dragged him out by the feet and laid him in a heap on the bank. Getting back onto his horse, he began to tell Alice about a new pudding he had invented which could be made with blotting paper, gunpowder, and sealing wax, which made Alice feel queer.

"And here I must leave you," said the White Knight. They had just come to the end of the wood.

Of all the strange things that Alice saw in her journey through the Looking-Glass, this was the one sight she would always remember most clearly. Years afterward, she could bring the whole scene back again, as if it had been only yesterday—the mild blue eyes and the kindly smile of the Knight; the setting sun gleaming through his hair and shining on his armor in a blaze of light that quite dazzled her; the horse moving about, with the reins hanging loose on his neck, cropping the grass at her feet.

The White Knight gathered up the reins and turned his horse's head along the road by which they had come.

"You've only a few yards to go," he told her, "down the hill and over that little brook and then you'll be a Queen."

Alice waved her handkerchief to the Knight to encourage him onward in his journey and waited till he was out of sight.

He asked her whether she would see him off and wave her handkerchief when he arrived at the turn in the road, to encourage him onward in his journey and say goodbye, to which Alice heartily agreed.

"Of course, I'll wait," said Alice affectionately. "And thank you for coming so far."

Thus, they shook hands and the Knight rode slowly away. Alice watched him as he yet again tumbled several times off his horse. Then she waved her handkerchief to him and waited till he was out of sight.

"I hope it encouraged him," she said as she turned to run down the hill. She threw herself into the lawn filled with blooming flowers and realized there was something on her head.

It was a golden crown.

"Well, this is really grand," said Alice. "I never expected I should be Queen so soon."

She got up and walked about with the crown on her head. At first, she walked rather stiffly, because she was afraid the crown would come off.

Suddenly, however, she found herself seated between the Red Queen and the White Queen.

But how did they come there? She wanted to know the answer, but then realized it might not be civil to ask.

"Speak when you're spoken to!" the Red Queen said sharply, as if she could read Alice's thoughts.

"But if everybody obeyed that rule," said Alice, "nobody would ever say anything at all."

"Ridiculous," cried the Red Queen, pooh-poohing Alice's grand remark.

The Red Queen then informed Alice that she would not be considered to be a Queen yet, until she passed certain tests.

"Always speak the truth—think before you speak and write it down afterward," said the Red Queen sharply, as she instructed Alice how to answer the test. There was an uncomfortable silence for a minute or two. The Red Queen broke the silence by saying to the White Queen, "I invite you to Alice's dinner party this afternoon."

The White Queen smiled feebly and said, "And I invite you."

Alice said that she didn't know she was to have a party at all, and even if she did, then in theory and for all practical purposes, it was she who was supposed to invite the guests and not the other two Queens.

The Red Queen was most annoyed with Alice and declared, "I daresay you've not had many lessons in manners yet."

The Red and the White Queen rain down a number of questions in arithmetic upon Alice.

"Manners are not taught in lessons," said Alice. "Lessons teach you to do sums and things of that sort."

This statement then made both the Red and the White Queen rain down a number of questions in arithmetic upon Alice: What's one plus one plus one plus one plus one plus one plus one? Subtract nine from eight. Divide a loaf by a knife.

And Alice couldn't answer all of these peculiar questions. She said to herself, "Oh what a lot of nonsense we are discussing."

"She can't do sums a bit!" the Queens said together with great emphasis.

"Can you do sums?" Alice tartly asked the White Queen, for she didn't at all like being found fault with so much.

The White Queen gasped and shut her eyes, saying that she could do addition if one gave her time but that she could not do subtraction at all.

"Fan her head!" the Red Queen anxiously interrupted and began to fan Alice with leaves. "She'll be feverish after so much thinking." So the Queens set to work and began to fan Alice with bunches of leaves, until poor Alice had to beg them to stop as it blew her hair about so much.

The Red Queen then told Alice that she should pat the tame White Queen on the head, but Alice refused to do so.

The White Queen, in her stead, gave a deep sigh and, laying her head on Alice's shoulder, she fell asleep.

"She's tired, poor thing," said the Red Queen, and soon she too fell asleep, leaning against Alice and snoring loudly.

"What am I to do?" exclaimed Alice, looking about at both the sleeping Queens, quite perplexed. "I don't think it ever happened before, that anyone had to take care of two sleeping Queens at once! Do wake up, you heavy things!" She went on in an impatient tone, but the only answer was gentle snoring.

Then, to Alice's great relief, the two giant heads suddenly vanished from her lap, and Alice was standing before an arched doorway over which the words, *Queen Alice* were written in large letters.

The door opened. Alice entered and saw that there were many guests sitting silently around in a large hall.

Alice glanced nervously along the table as she walked up the large hall. She noticed there were about fifty guests of various kinds, some were animals, some were birds, and some were even flowers.

There were three chairs at the head of the table. The Red Queen and the White Queen had already taken two of them, but the middle one was empty. Alice sat down in it.

"You've missed the soup and fish," the Red Queen sternly informed Alice. "Put on the joint!" she called out loudly.

The waiters set a leg of mutton before Alice, who looked at it rather anxiously as she had never had to carve a joint of mutton before.

"Let me introduce you to that leg of mutton," said the Red Queen, pointing to the leg of mutton. "Alice, this is Mutton; Mutton, this is Alice."

The leg of mutton got up in the dish and made a little bow to Alice. Alice returned the bow, not knowing whether to be frightened or amused.

"May I give you a slice?" Alice said, taking up the knife and fork and looking from one Queen to the other.

"Certainly not," the Red Queen said gruffly. "It isn't etiquette or good manners to cut anyone you've just been introduced to. Remove the joint!"

The waiters carried it off and brought a large plum pudding in its place.

"I don't want to be introduced to the pudding please," said Alice rather hastily, "or we shall get no dinner at all."

But the Red Queen still introduced Alice to the pudding, and then she ordered the pudding to be taken away. With great effort, Alice overcame her shyness and gave the order to bring back the pudding.

The leg of mutton got up in the dish and made a little bow to Alice.

Then she cut a slice of the pudding and handed it to the Red Queen.

"What impertinence!" said the pudding. "I wonder how you'd like it if I were to cut a slice out of you!" And all that Alice could do was sit and gasp at it.

The Red Queen raised a toast to Alice, whom she addressed as "Queen Alice," at the top of her voice. The guests raised their glasses and began to attack the food rather disgustingly. What with the guests acting so terribly, and the Red Queen and the White Queen squeezing Alice in between way too much, Alice was fed up.

"I can't stand this any longer!" she cried as she jumped up and seized the tablecloth with both hands. One good pull, and plates, dishes, guests and candles came crashing down together in a heap on the floor.

"And as for you," Alice grabbed the Red Queen, whom she thought to be the reason for all the mischief, "I'm going to shake you, till you turn into a kitten; that I will."

And the Red Queen began to shrink right before Alice's eyes—and turned into the BLACK KITTEN!

Alice was convinced that in her dream, and it was a grand dream too, that the black kitten had been the Red

Queen and Snowdrop, the white kitten, had been the White Queen, but none would own up to it.

Even the older cat, Dinah, did nothing else but clean the white kitten.

AVAILABLE TITLES

The Legend of Sleepy Hollow
by Washington Irving

Through the Looking-Glass
And What Alice Found There
by Lewis Carroll

FORTHCOMING TITLES

Carmilla
By Joseph Sheridan Le Fanu

The Canterville Ghost
by Oscar Wilde

Rip Van Winkle
by Washington Irving

Daddy-Long-Legs
by Jean Webster

Diary of a Nobody
by George and Weedon Grossmith

Agnes Grey
by Anne Bronte

The Picture of Dorian Gray
by Oscar Wilde

These titles, and many more, have been specially abridged by authors Fiza Pathan and Michaelangelo Zane for children aged seven to twelve. These books will introduce children to the rich repertory of rare classic literature which has not been abridged before now.

We invite you to subscribe to our email list so that you will know when new titles become available.

Email: fizapathan@fizapathanpublishing.com
Website: http://fizapathanpublishing.org/

9 788193 820100